No Valentines
for Katie

by Fran Manushkin

illustrated by Tammie Lyon

PICTURE WINDOW BOOKS
a capstone imprint

Katie Woo is published by Picture Window Books,
151 Good Counsel Drive, P.O. Box 669
Mankato, Minnesota, MN 56002
www.capstonepub.com

Text © 2011 Fran Manushkin
Illustrations © 2011 Picture Window Books

Library of Congress Cataloging-in-Publication Data is
available on the Library of Congress website.
ISBN: 978-1-4048-5986-9 (library binding)
ISBN: 978-1-4048-6365-1 (paperback)

Summary: Katie feels sad when she does not get a
valentine during her school Valentine's Day party.

Art Director: Kay Fraser
Graphic Designer: Emily Harris

Photo Credits
Fran Manushkin, pg. 26
Tammie Lyon, pg. 26

Table of Contents

Chapter 1
Counting Hearts

It was a cold gray day,

but Katie was happy. It was

Valentine's Day!

At school, Miss Winkle

said, "Let's start the day with

a valentine math puzzle."

"Take out your crayons, and draw a big heart. Then try to guess how many candy hearts will fit inside of it."

Katie drew a big red

heart. Then she looked at the

tiny candy hearts.

One said, "Puppy Love."

Another said, "Melt

My Heart."

"I think this heart will

hold twelve candies," Katie

decided. But when she filled

up the heart, it held twenty.

"Boy, did I guess wrong!"

Katie said.

"I love these tiny hearts,"

she said, smiling.

She couldn't stop reading

them. She read "Cloud Nine"

and "Soul Mate."

Miss Winkle said, "Now print your name on a piece of paper, and put it in the valentine box."

Then the class went out for recess.

Chapter 2
Making Valentines

When they came back,

Miss Winkle said, "Now the

real fun starts!"

"Take out a piece of paper from the valentine box. You will make a valentine for the person that you pick," said Miss Winkle.

Katie picked Barry, the new boy.

As Katie began painting, Miss Winkle said, "Each valentine should say something nice about the person."

Katie whispered to JoJo,
"I wonder who made me a
valentine? I can't wait to see
what it says about me!"

Ella read her card first.

"This valentine is for Pedro.

I like you because you are a

great goalie! When we play

soccer, you know how to use

your head!"

"Thanks!"

Pedro said.

Charlotte read her valentine. "JoJo, I like you because you jump rope so fast! And when I forget to bring my lunch, you share yours with me."

"Thank you!" said JoJo, beaming.

Chapter 3
A Valentine for Katie

One by one, the students

read their valentines. But

nobody read one for Katie.

Katie's eyes filled with tears. "Someone got my name," she said, "but I guess they couldn't think of anything nice to say. That's why I didn't get a card."

"Katie," said Miss Winkle,

"are you sure you put your

name into the box?"

"Oh, no!" Katie groaned.

"I forgot! I was so busy

reading my candy hearts."

"Well," said Miss Winkle,
"since Katie did not get a
card, will someone come
up to the board and write
something nice about her?"

"I will!" said Barry, the

new boy.

He wrote, "I think Katie is

very funny. And her glasses

are just like mine!"

Katie smiled. "Thank

you!" she said.

Now Barry looked sad.

"I didn't get a card," he said.

Katie jumped up. "I got

your name!" she said.

"Barry, I don't know you very well, but I think you are funny! Plus you have the same glasses as me!"

Barry couldn't stop smiling. "Katie, we said the same things!"

After school, Katie said, "Barry, can you walk home with us?"

"Sure," he agreed. "Do you promise to be funny?"

"I always am!" said Katie.

And they laughed together all the way home.

About the Author

Fran Manushkin is the author of many popular picture books, including *How Mama Brought the Spring; Baby, Come Out!; Latkes and Applesauce: A Hanukkah Story;* and *The Tushy Book.* There is a real Katie Woo — she's Fran's great-niece — but she never gets in half the trouble of the Katie Woo in the books. Fran writes on her beloved Mac computer in New York City, without the help of her two naughty cats, Cookie and Goldy.

About the Illustrator

Tammie Lyon began her love for drawing at a young age while sitting at the kitchen table with her dad. She continued her love of art and eventually attended the Columbus College of Art and Design, where she earned a bachelors degree in fine art. After a brief career as a professional ballet dancer, she decided to devote herself full time to illustration. Today she lives with her husband, Lee, in Cincinnati, Ohio. Her dogs, Gus and Dudley, keep her company as she works in her studio.

Glossary

amazed (uh-MAZED)—very surprised

beaming (BEEM-ing)—smiling very widely

goalie (GOH-lee)—the person who guards the goal in soccer to keep the other team from scoring

groaned (GROHND)—made a long, low sound to show unhappiness

recess (REE-sess)—a break from school

soul (SOLE)—a part of a person that you cannot see; some people believe that the soul controls feelings and thoughts

Valentine's Day (VAL-uhn-tines DAY)—February 14, a day named in honor of Saint Valentine. It is celebrated by sharing cards called valentines.

Discussion Questions

1. What is your favorite part of Valentine's Day?

2. Katie felt disappointed when she did not get a valentine. Have you ever felt disappointed? What happened?

3. Katie and Barry had the same glasses. Do you and one of your classmates have something that matches, like the same shirt or shoes? What is it?

Writing Prompts

1. Write down three facts that you know about Valentine's Day. If you can't think of three, ask a grown-up to help you find some in a book or on the computer.

2. Make a valentine for someone else. Be sure to write a special message just for them.

3. What would you have written in a valentine for Katie? Write it down.

Cooking with Katie

Valentine's Day is the perfect day to cook something special for the people you love. Here is an easy recipe that will go with any Valentine's Day dinner. Before you get started, ask a grown-up for help, and don't forget to wash your hands!

Behold-My-Heart Breadsticks
*Makes 12 breadsticks

Ingredients:

- 1 can of refrigerated breadsticks
- 1 egg, beaten
- 2 tablespoons Parmesan cheese

Other things you need:

- a large cookie sheet
- a pastry brush
- a spoon

What you do:

1. Preheat the oven to 375 degrees.

2. Separate the breadstick dough into 12 pieces. Stretch each piece until it is 12 inches long.

3. Shape each piece into a heart. Pinch the ends together. Place the heart on the cookie sheet.

4. With the pastry brush, brush your hearts with the beaten egg.

5. With the spoon, shake a little Parmesan cheese on the top of each heart.

6. Bake for 10 to 13 minutes, or until golden brown.

To make it extra yummy, try dipping your heart in warm pizza sauce. Enjoy!

WAIT!

Don't close the book!
There's more!

- Learn more about Katie and her friends

- Find a Katie Woo color sheet, scrapbook, and stationary

- Discover more Katie Woo books

All at . . .

www.capstonekids.com

Still want more?

Find cool websites and more books like this one at www.FACTHOUND.com.

Just type in the **BOOK ID:** 9781404859869 and you're ready to go!